This one's for me

Published by Two Lions, New York • www.apub.com
Amazon, the Amazon logo, and Two Lions are trademarks of Amazon.com, Inc., or its affiliates.

ISBN-13: 9781542043403 • ISBN-10: 1542043409
The illustrations were created digitally.
Book design by Abby Dening • Printed in China

First Edition • 10 9 8 7 6 5 4 3 2 1

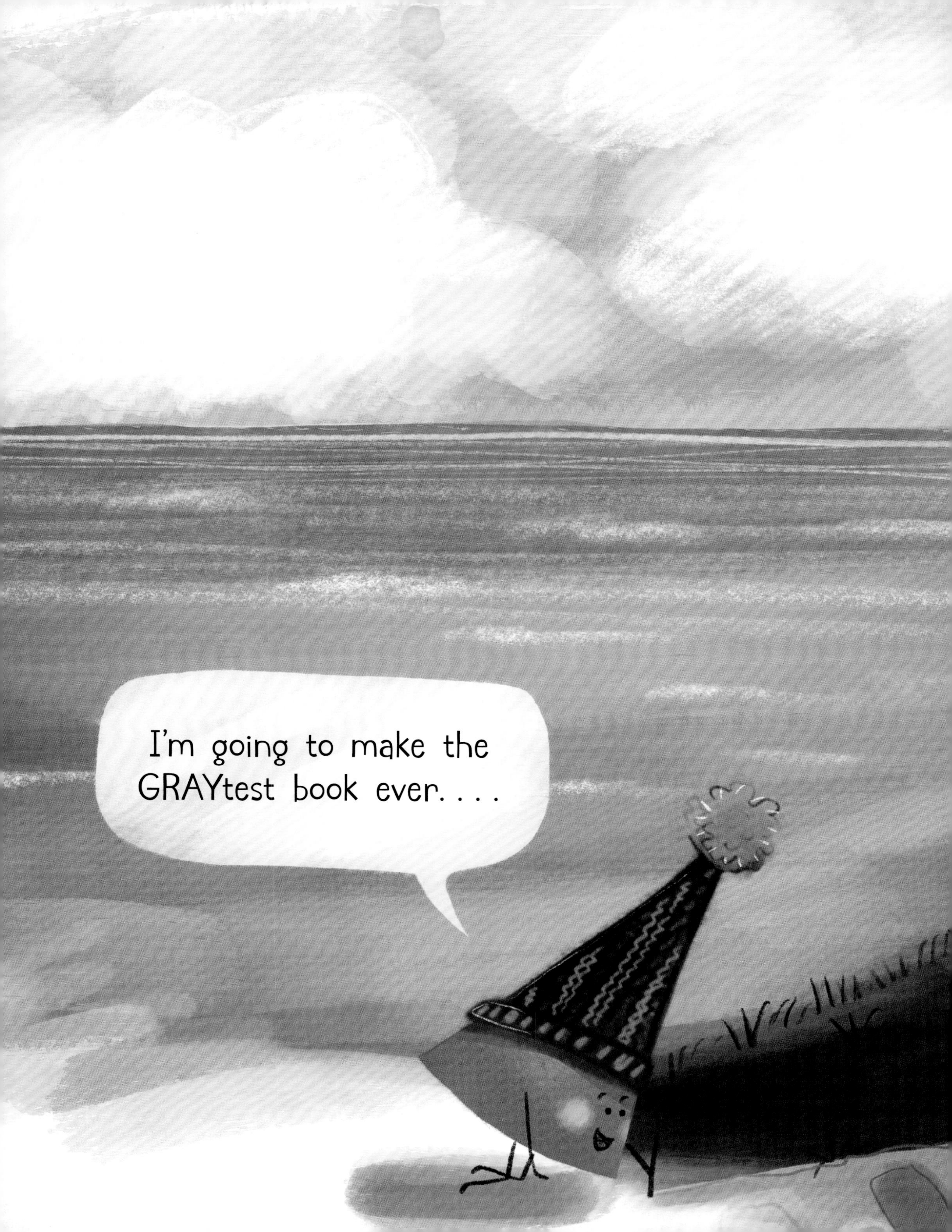
I'm going to make the GRAYtest book ever. . . .

Once upon a time, a wolf, a kitten, and a hippo lived in a small house by the sea. (Some would describe the house as dismal, bleak, or gloomy.)

But it wasn't. It was lovely.
And GRAY.
And perfect.

Hey, Gray, what are you doin'?
I'm telling a story. . . .
This looks dismal, bleak, and gloomy.
Yeah, this is kind of depressing. . . .
It's just a little overcast. Perfect weather if you ask me. . . .

But you can't illustrate a good story without the Primary colors!
Yeah, the three of us are, like, really important. Everyone loves us!

The wolf, the kitten, and the hippo . . .

Is the wolf going to EAT the kitten? Because I feel like that's where this is going.

*Sigh. Of course not! Just because this book is gray doesn't mean it's scary or sad.

So, like, what are these animals going to eat if they don't have a proper sun? It certainly won't be organic.
I'm guessing the kitten.
Do you mind? I'm trying to tell my story here. . . .

Hey, what's everyone arguing about?

Hey, Secondaries. We're discussing Gray's monochromatic disaster.

It's about, like, a totally cute kitten who gets eaten by a wolf.

Okay... but what's with the hippo?
Yeah, dude, we're not sure how he fits in either.
Ooh, a kitten!
Is anyone listening to me? I said no Primaries and no Secondaries! This book is GRAY!
What muted his hue?
Can I *please* get back to my story?

One day the wolf decided to host a brunch. . . .

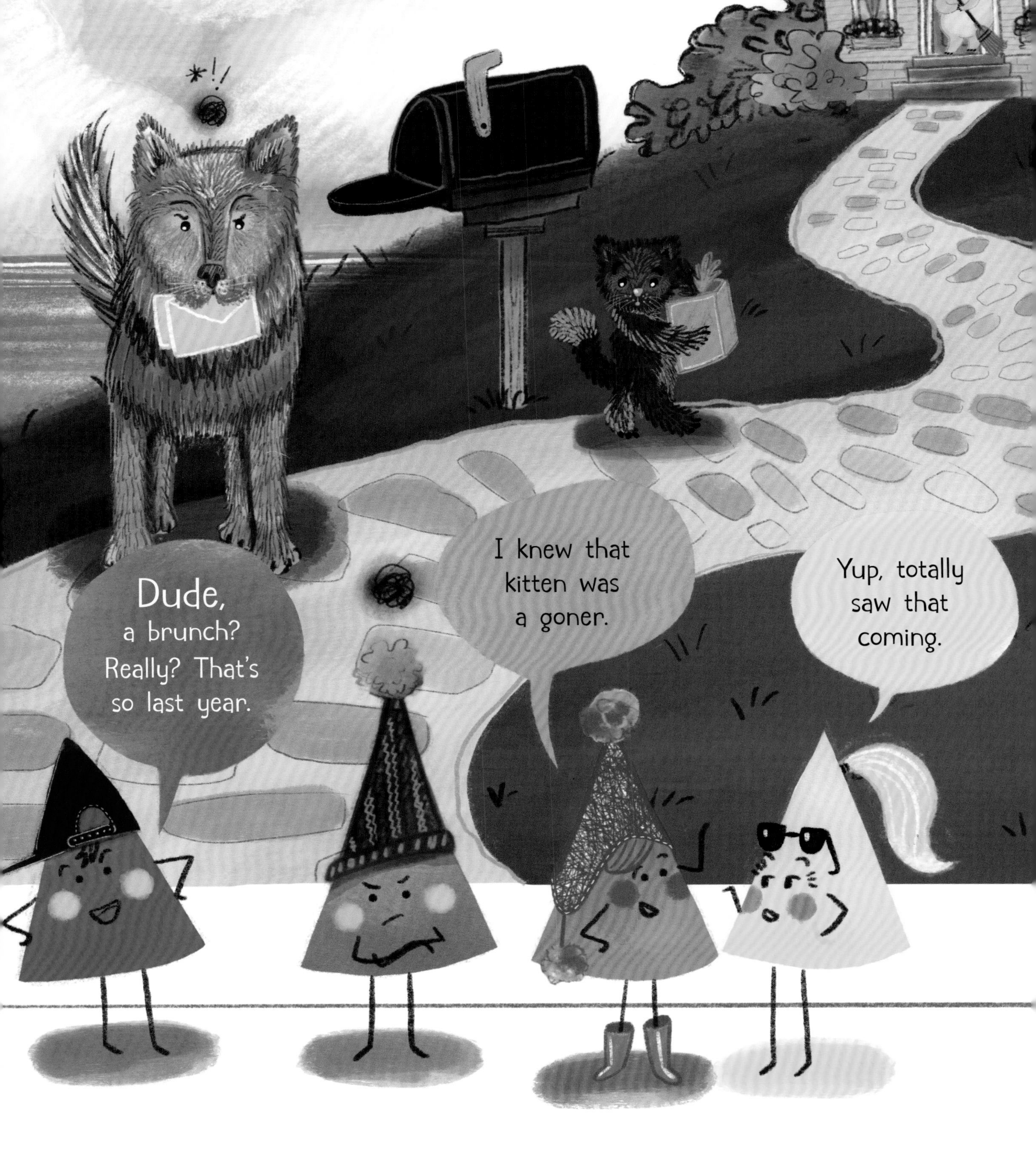

Well, White and I are achromatic, just like you. So . . . can we be in your book?

Sorry, guys, this book is gray. But maybe— White, what are you doing?!

The wolf was just about to pull the scones out
of the oven when . . .

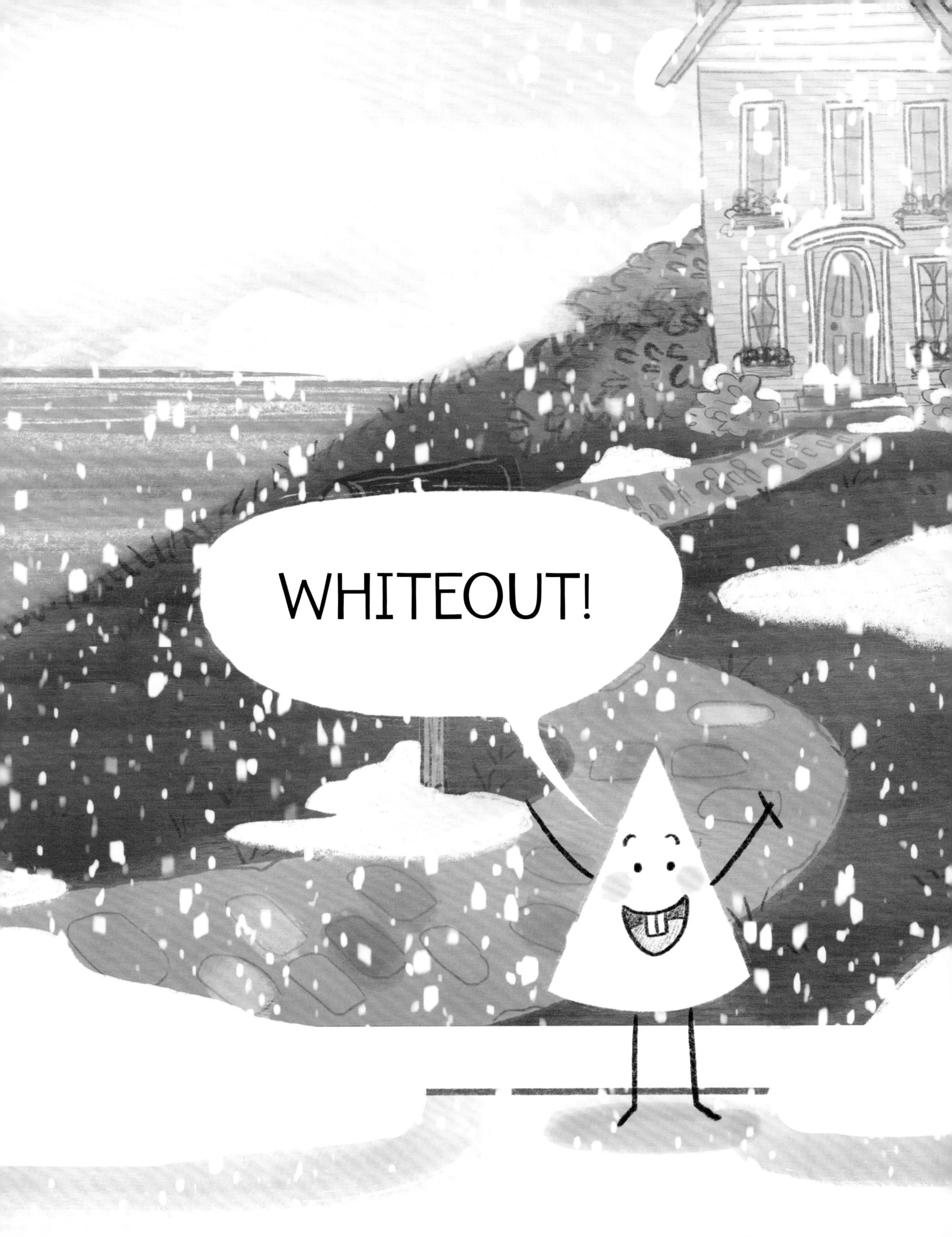
WHITEOUT!

NO, NO, NO!
THIS BOOK IS GRAY
LIKE ME!

WHY IS THAT SO HARD TO UNDERSTAND?
YOU GUYS GET TO BE IN EVERYTHING.
I'M LEFT OUT ALL THE TIME.
I DON'T EVEN GET
TO BE IN THE RAINBOW!
I JUST WANTED TO SHOW YOU WHAT
I CAN DO.... GRAY IS A COOL
COLOR, TOO, YOU KNOW?!

*Sigh
I just get tired of being the one no one wants to color with. . . . Everyone thinks I'm dull . . . but I can be bold. I can be interesting too.

Sorry, Gray. I got a little carried away there.
Yeah, man, we're sorry.
Sometimes we can be a little off-color.

How am I going to get rid of all this snow?! This book is supposed to be GRAY. But now it's ruined.
No worries, Gray, we can, like, totally help you fix this. . . . That is, if you want us to.

Even though the wolf's scones burned
due to an unexpected weather delay,
all the guests had a lovely time together
in the garden. It was a great party.

Ta-da!
Isn't it, like,
totally awesome?!
And look, we got
Brown and Pink
to help us!

Dude!
Gray is such
a cool color!
I don't know
how we never
noticed before.

Look at
all these
GRAY
animals!

WOW!
This book is gray . . .
AND colorful! I love it!

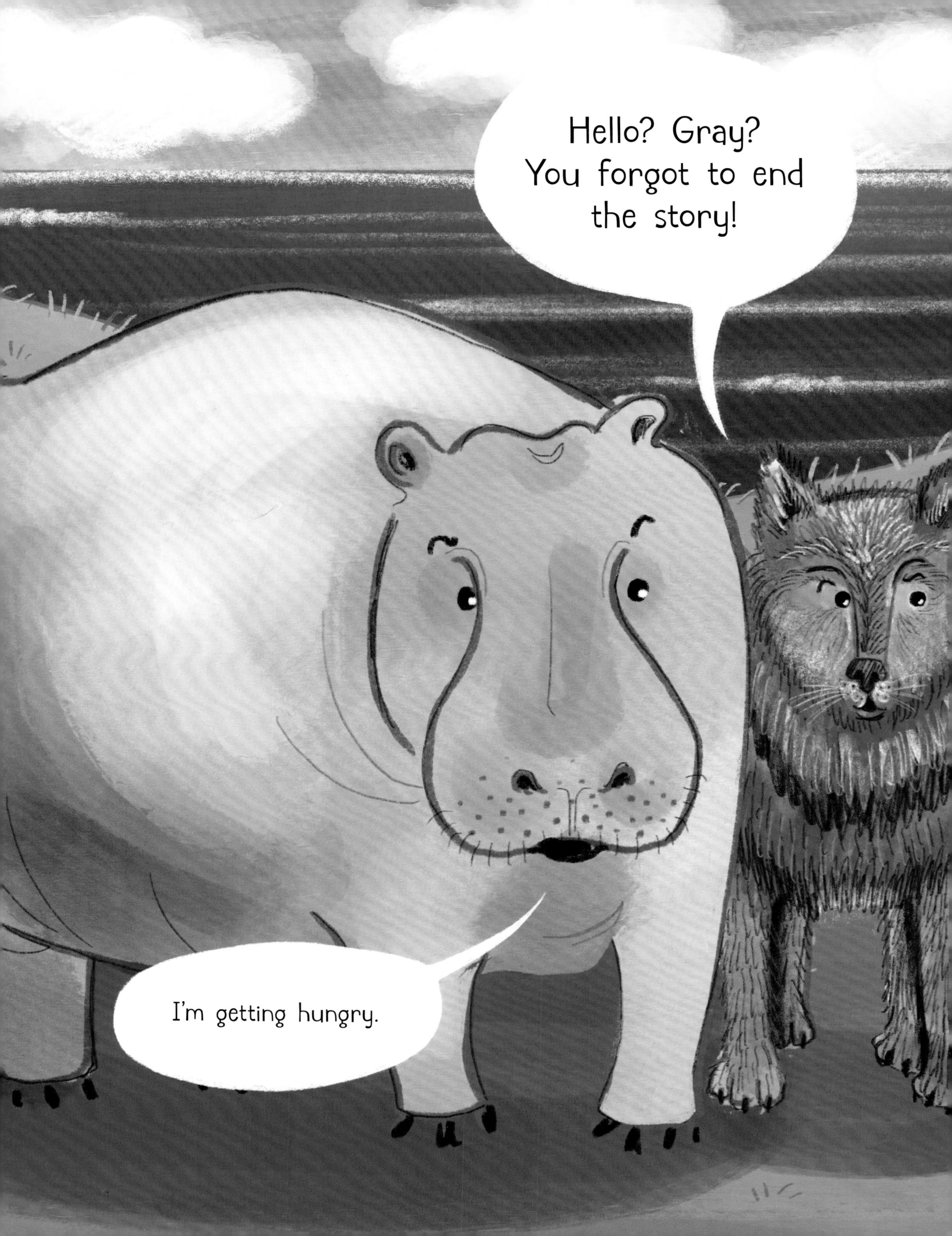
Hello? Gray? You forgot to end the story!
I'm getting hungry.

Sorry, guys!
I was coloring
with my friends.
I'm almost done. . . .

Turns out the kitten
could whip up a mean
brunch. Oh, and they
lived grayly ever after.

THE END